AS A MAN THINKETH

AS A MAN THINKETH

By

Norah Currer

HERMES

2 Tavistock Chambers, Bloomsbury Way, London WC1A 2SE

First Published 1995

ISBN 1 86032 030 9

Typesetting by Phil Hine

Made and printed in Great Britain by M.B.C, Ipswich, Great Britain

ACKNOWLEDGEMENTS

Norah Currer with her husband Bill, not only opened up their home to bring the teaching of Spirit to the many who came to their sanctuary of peace (The White Chapel - see p51), but also worked hard on the healing side to help those who were in distress - in both worlds.
I am very pleased to arrange publication, so readers can also be aware of these teachings.

Bernard Deerlove

FOREWORD

It is the Power of Thought that governs and determines the Path and design of our lives. As Jesus said "The greatest Power in Heaven and Earth is the Power of Thought." No matter what we do, or create, it is first formed in the mind, whether it be good or otherwise. A thought is not something gone or forgotten, it is a powerful living vibration, that can be stored in the subconscious mind, and will not only remain there, during our lifetime on Earth, but be a part of our life when we depart, and return to our real Home in the World of Spirit. There it will still influence our life, until we find a deep peace, and all material thoughts of the past life are erased.
The few examples recorded here will show how the powerful mind controls, by its acceptance of what we have learned, accepted and stored within the life span. Perhaps a life which has been given in service to mankind, but governed by wrong teachings, so not quite within the "Father's Laws," Perfect Laws, which never change, and we can only find if we seek within. The Father within, the Kingdom of Heaven within. Life is full of lessons to be learned, that is our purpose of this Life, all geared towards our Spiritual advancement. Every Life is a stepping stone towards the ultimate perfection of the Spirit.

These Life Stories brought by Souls who have returned to Spirit, have been recorded and brought to us by our beloved highly developed Medium. Souls we have been able to converse with, and who do indeed convey the Power of Thought, bringing much realisation to us.

I trust you will find the stories of these Souls Lives, not only interesting, but inspiring to seek the truth of Life Eternal NOW.

JESUS taught "SEEK AND YOU SHALL FIND, KNOCK AND IT SHALL BE OPENED UNTO YOU."

If you truly seek, you will be guided to find the anwers to your questions, and a peaceful, much more beneficial way of Life here and now.

A positive progress Materially and Spiritually.

GOD BLESS YOU IN YOUR SEEKING AND ACCEPTANCE.

ONE

These stories are of Souls who have returned to God's Kingdom, with minds filled and obsessed with the life they have left behind Without correct teachings or understanding, often failing to realise that they have passed over, so are unwilling to leave earthly conditions behind.

In some cases where there has been a rejection of the Father God and a very negative or violent life, they will be in different degrees of darkness, really a darkness of the mind, and can remain this way for eons of years in our time. Spirit Guides are constantly trying to help, but the minds are closed, and they will not listen. There will eventually come a time, when they begin to realise something is wrong and ask for help, which will be there immediately, in the form of Light and Guidance.

There are Souls who have lived good, kindly lives, in service to others, but have been misguided in their religious teachings, and need to make contact with the Earth again, through a rescue circle, controlled by an advanced Spiritual Medium, and his or her control. There we are able to speak to them, as they are allowed to control the medium, and are able to eventually bring Light and Peace of mind to them. Usually, after acceptance, resting and finding complete peace of mind, they will express a desire to serve the Father God, helping to correct the same errors in other Souls.

The Father God working through his children. We can all learn much through these children's experiences, and acceptance of the lives they lived.

The important message brought here, is, that all should know that, *LIFE IS ETERNAL*. All disbelievers will find this to be a fact. As all must experience the transition from the earthly life to the Spiritual, which is our *real* life. This is not something to be feared, there is no pain in leaving this earth plane. It should be peaceful, and like passing from one room to another.

Not understanding God s perfect laws, many believe that when so called death has taken place, there is nothing, one is finished, so it is sometimes difficult to persuade a Soul they are alive, and able to converse with us.

We have experienced many cases of a dear old lady, whose husband has long since left her; just sitting alone, maybe sewing, knitting or reading; who will be adamant she has not died. She can hear us and talk to us, and will take a lot of persuasion about the.beautiful life awaiting her, where her loved one is waiting. Of course, she becomes overjoyed when realisation takes place, and she becomes re-united with her dear one.
Similarly, some Souls may have passed at home, and are crippled in some way, perhaps a severe affliction has taken them, or they may have lost limbs. These Souls are still in the same state mentally, and are most distressed. It is only when they become healed through the Power of Prayer or through the Power of Jesus, that they begin to realise the truth of their passing. As they are made whole, they are told of the Life of Perfection and Beauty that awaits them in the Father's Kingdom.
Souls that have been disfigured in this Life and sometimes treated cruelly because of their condition, once released from that mis-shapen body, by Prayer and Healing, their minds then reject the earthly condition, and become perfect. It is such a joy to see the happiness and gratitude to Father God, when they also accept that they took on this form in life, to understand the condition and suffering that takes place being in a disfigured-condition and, especially, the great Spiritual progress they have made through it all. Life's purpose is to learn and make Spiritual Progress through the earth life.
Another lady who had passed over in hospital, was so distressed because she saw someone else in the bed, and could not understand why no one took any notice of her. It took a little convincing as to what had happened to her, to accept and go her way, in Perfection and Healed, into the wonderful life awaiting her.
When we speak to one such Soul, she becomes the spokes woman for many similar cases, wha are also listening, brought by their Guides (also often referred to as Guardian Angels). Receiving the same help and responding.
The most difficult to convince, are the big businessman used to controlling everything and everyone. So big and important are they in their own minds, that they have no need of the Father God, and think they can do everything all by themselves. Often with little regard for anyone else or, as to the methods used to make money. Perhaps they suffered a sudden heart attack and passed on without being aware it was so. They become so frustrated and angry because no one is carrying out their orders, or

even listening to them. When brought to a Rescue Circle and confronted with their predicament, these people are adamant in their denial that death could possibly have happened, the business cannot be left, saying they must go back to control it. Of course, they also decide that,God has no right to take them away, so will find themselves in darkness, until becoming humble and praying for help. It usually takes some time to penetrate a mind so completely possessed with only material gain. Eventually, all will come to Father God. He is the Light and Life within, by which we have Life.

TWO

THE LIFE OF A SOUTH AFRICAN FARM BOY

Good evening, my name is Bennie, I lived in your country and in a home where the bible or, as my Father used to call it, 'God s words, the good book.' Every night he reads the bible to us and we go to church every Sunday.

We lived on a farm and, although, we knew that God created us and God made the world and that we must be good, my father said, whenever we did anything wrong, we would be punished by God s wrath.

From a child, I could only think of God s wrath and if I did anything wrong I tried to hide for I feared this God and his wrath. I went to church with my parents, but I feared my father's wrath more than I did God's wrath, as did all the servants who worked for my father, for he was so quick with his whip.

We knew by the scorn of our father s voice, when it was time to run and even our black men ran, so it was that I was afraid of God's wrath and I was afraid of my father's wrath and, my mother, she too, was afraid of my father's wrath.

Sunday was the day of rest and we must do no work, for it was God s day and, on this day, we must appease God by going to church. This was my life, our farm was far away from any town and we had no motor cars to take us about, but we had a tractor on the farm which was my father's pride and joy.

One day I took this tractor to work in the fields and part of the farm was on a hill; I cannot remember why, but the tractor fell over and when I saw what had happened, I ran and hid in a klompie of bushes. I was too scared to go home and waited in the bushes. When I saw my father and the labourers came and looked at the tractor, I could see that my father was very upset and I watched him return to the house. He returned with my mother and they looked at the tractor and I saw them crying because the tractor was broken and not worrying about me or wondering where I was. I stayed in the bushes and could see the people coming to the house. I knew it was time to go and face my father's wrath, even though he was not worrying about me or wondering where I was.

I went to the house and saw my mother in the kitchen and spoke to her, she took no notice of me and I pulled her dress and said "Mamma, I am sorry". She took no notice. I went to my father for he would have to get out the whip. I told myself not to be afraid. I said, 'Papa, I am sorry", and he looked right through me, so I told him that I did not mind and that he could thrash me. I was sorry that I had broken the tractor; he took no notice as he was crying and everyone was crying. I thought to myself that it was all because I had broken the tractor.

I went back to the bushes and thought to myself; who can help me, to whom can I go and say, "I am sorry". Then I remembered my Oom Piet. I had a great love for my Oom Piet, but he was dead. At that moment, I could see my Oom Piet coming towards me and I forgot that he was dead and I said, "Oom Piet, look, it broke and now my mother and father don't want to see me, they don't want to know me, and they are crying all the time for this tractor". Oom Piet said to me, "Bennie, you are like me now" and I said, "How do you mean, I am like you? You are dead, am I dead too?"

I was frightened, I did not want to be dead and I thought of God's wrath. I cried and I screamed, "I do not want to be dead' I am afraid of God and I am afraid of my father. Where am I going?" Oom Piet said to me, "God is not angry with you, God does not get angry with you". I replied, "You tell me that when in the good book, the Bible, it says always of God's wrath, all must be good because of God's wrath. You have got to face that when you die". He said, "No, you must come with me. I will take you to the house first". There I saw my mother who was still crying and she was standing next to a photograph of me. He said to me, "They are not crying because the tractor is broken, they are crying because you are dead".

Oom Piet took me and showed me God's country, but I was so full of fear for I had been told that when you have done wrong, you must be punished and now Oom Piet told me there is no punishment. He took me to a beautiful farm and said this is where I would stay for a little bit; it is all beautiful and I forgot all about being frightened.

Oom Piet took me to another place with lots of people and they were all wearing bright clothes of different colours. He said, "I will leave you

now and you will come back to me when you are ready". I was with these people and I think they prayed. I cannot remember, but I felt as though I had received a most wonderful shower, I felt clean, I felt light and I was not frightened anymore. They said, "Bennie, you were taught wrong things. You were never taught about love, you were never taught that you must control your emotions, that no man should get so angry that he can raise his hand to someone else in anger. You will have to pray for your father for he made so many people cry."
That is how I came to find my peace and to see how many now come through God's country as I did, and this is where I try to work, to help these people to find this beautiful peace, to become clean and light and love everything and everybody. This is how it is, and I ask you to find this love and help everybody.

Is your father with you now?
He is resting, I suppose you know.
In a sanatorium?

He is in a sanatorium and he has his dog beside him, so when he wakes he will see this dog which he thrashed sometimes and he will realise that this dog still loves him.

THREE

THE STORY OF EMMA

I am going to tell you a story about a Soul who lived on your earth plane many years ago. Like so many when you are young and have plans for the future, things that you hope you will be able to do whether it be painting, music or writing; you want to be someone great, you want to have your name known.

Somewhere in each and every child is an ambition and, as in this Soul as a child, whom we shall call by the name of Emma, from her school days, she desired to be a writer of books, to bring joy and happiness to all people, to write books that would bring laughter.

Emma had been so tired of reading the dull books that she had had in the class rooms during her school days, she carried this thought at the back of her mind that this was what she wanted to do, but there came a time when, because of financial difficulties, she had to leave school and take a position in a home where she became a nurse maid and cook.

All the time she was working in this home, she began to feel frustrated and upset, she knew she had to do her work well because her employers were strict and she also needed the money. She could not just walk out and all the time she was working, she knew she was pleasing the Madam. This frustration began to build up into bitterness and hate. Why should she be like this when she wanted to be a writer? She wanted to give something to the world, not only to this family with whom she lived and worked, but to all. These vibrations began to build up until she became irritable with her employers, because in those days, it was not the place for employers to find out what makes the underlings and their servants happy or unhappy.

One day, in sheer desperation, everything seemed to go wrong and Emma walked out. She did not know where she was going, but said, "I hate what I am doing. I hate the people I work for and I never get out, I never meet people, I never go places where I can find someone,

someone that I can open myself to. I want to write, I must write," not realising that with the little education she had she would never be able to write a book.

As Emma walked along the street, she noticed some people standing outside a hall and because she had nowhere to go she walked in. Inside a man was speaking and he was telling them that some people felt confined in the work they do, they may think they could do better elsewhere and become frustrated, but if they prayed, as they have the Father God consciously in and around them, they would know that what they were doing, they were doing for the Father.

She stayed behind when all the others had left and she went to this man and said, "You spoke very kindly. You made me feel you were speaking to me," and she poured out all her problems; what she wanted to do and what she had to do for she had no other way of earning money. The advice this man gave to her, "I give to you now." He said to Emma, "You know you have God in you." Emma thought for a moment and said, "Yes." You are working at a hot stove, you are feeling the heat and you are feeling depressed, now remember, "God in me." Try to bless the food that the others will eat, why not see God in everything that you have to do for you are working for God. This is what you chose to do, to work for God, so now try to see God in everything.

It was late when she returned to her place of employment in the morning and she was wondering whether she would be given notice because of her outburst the previous day. She thought to herself, God in me, God in you, at that moment she happened to look out of the window and it was raining and, previously, the first thought that would have flashed through her mind would have been, "Oh, what a miserable day," and she would have gone downstairs in misery

Emma looked outside and saw the rain falling on the trees, on the streets, the gardens and flowers. This was her first lesson, she looked out and said "God in you, God in me. He has brought rain to clean you, refresh you". She felt so uplifted, she walked down the stairs to the kitchen and said to herself, "God in me, God in you. I work for God in me and God in you and everything." She became so much brighter, the dishes she prepared were beautiful and she felt uplifted to see what she had managed to do for her employers. She took the food through to the dining-room and before she thought of yesterday, she thought of God in you, God in me, and she smiled.

Madam came to her and said, "Good morning Emma. Thank you for the beautiful breakfast and I hope you will not leave us. We love you, you have worked for so long with us and if there is anything we can do to make you happy, will you please let us know." From then on she brought this affirmation God in me, God in you. Her whole life changed. She did start a book and every day she wrote of all the times she had found happiness, pleasure and joy and that book became her light and life.
Although no one ever read the book, it was what it did for her; the radiance that shone from within to without that attracted so many to her and this is how she told God in me, God in you, God in everyone and God in everything.
I ask you to take this now into your life, for you are told, "The Father and I are one." In times of frustration when you feel that the material world has nothing to offer you and you wonder what the future holds, the uncertainty of the unknown, know my friends, "The Father and I are one." God in me therefore I see God in everything. GOD IS LOVE and this is what little Emma did she was talking to people of love, she had love, everyone had love and in giving out love you attract love to you.

In all things try to follow the way of peace and each one of you will be a channel of peace and you will see and you will do and you will think and say only those things that will make peace. I ask please think of yourselves as peacemakers, for being peacemakers you are being channels for the Father God. With peace comes love, friendship and happiness.
I hope you enjoy your festive season and I hope you give to many people these thoughts, God in you, God in me. We need to only know that nothing else matters, other than "The Father and I are one." He sees to all things, He knows your needs, knows your problems. He knows what the future holds for you and when you find the peace which is in you, only then will He be able to make everything in your life a joy, a thing of beauty, a thing of peace and wonder, that all might love you.
Be grateful for knowing that they might be able to follow the examples you have set them and you do this so unconsciously, because you are radiating peace and the Christ Love.
I bless you all, may the joy of this festive season remain with you for not only one day, but every day of the following year and for every year until eternity. "GOD IN YOU, GOD IN ME."

So I bless you in the name of the Father, the Son and the Holy Spirit. Go in your beautiful peace and love.

FOUR

MONEY BAGS

Here is a fascinating story of one, whom we have named "money bags."
With understanding, some of the rescue cases can be either amusing or pathetic, all, however, clearly demonstrate how the all-powerful mind controls all of life. When used correctly, the mind can produce and achieve a positive, masterful and balanced way, materially and spiritually, a progressive rewarding life span.
Our friend "money bags" was allowed to control the Medium and was in a great state of exuberance and misery scooping up money and jewels from a hugh pile, letting it filter through his fingers with exclamations of joy, continually repeating the process in his mind. So absorbed was he with his riches and completely oblivious to anything else, not even aware he had left the earth.
His lust for power and greed of gain, was all absorbing, as it had been during his life, a very selfish life. He was completely engrossed in his earthly possessions. After having talked to him for about an hour, he filled his bag, placed it over his shoulder, and went his way.
With a mind so filled with only this thought of possessions, he could roam around with his loot for thousands of years, in our time, quite happy within himself. Many High Spirits had already tried to persuade him, that the gold was only in his mind.
He had had no love in his life, was one of a family of five and always had a very real obsession to be wealthy, to accumulate huge amounts of money. "Money bags" had a business, not run on straight and honest lines. He 'did' people out of money in his dealings with them. The more money he had, the more he wanted, he was constantly grabbing.
One day he fell down a flight of stairs, breaking his neck. This happened so suddenly, and his only thought was for his money, his gold. Still his, mentally, no one was allowed to touch it. Of course, he alone was able

to see it, as no one takes material possessions with them from the earth plane. In his own words, he was quite proud to say he had snitched his money from other people, to have gambled and cheated.

When he first came to speak to us, he would not stay long, he was afraid that we would steal his gold. It was difficult at times for him always having to carry it around, for fear of it being stolen. He could not place it in any security, likewise there was the Receiver of Revenue.

Eventually, after much time had elapsed, he began to realise there was a greater power than gold. Walking great distances with his gold, unable to see the great beauty of the Father's Kingdom, in darkness only seeing the gold, various High Spiritual Guides continued to try to enlighten him, including his own Guide. One time as he was walking, a very beautiful lady appeared to him and asked where he was going and where he came from. "London Town," was the answer. The beautiful Lady Miriam said, "Oh that was a very long time ago." He did not wish to argue, being very impressed, as she was so beautiful, he just had to keep walking, having nowhere to live.

Lady Miriam took him to see two houses, one a big beautiful house, the other a broken down old place. On enquiring if he liked the big house, replied, "Oh yes indeed."

"That is because your mind is so set on riches," said Miriam. He said, that that was because he had been a poor man all his life and wanted security. Miriam then explained that the owner of the mansion was a poor man, whilst the old tumbled down house belonged to a rich man. This was of course very difficult for him to understand. She explained that the man living in the old house had made money his God, having spent millions on his home, gloating over his money. There can only be one God, and "money bags" realised that he too had made money his God.

The poor man, now living in the mansion, knew that there was God the Father, and did not blame Him for the condition he had found himself in. aware that it was a portion of his life he had to experience to know how to beg, to be humble, to be completely satisfied with what was given to him, even a dry crust. He bore no malice, no hatred towards humanity sending out only love and pity to those that did not understand.

So "money bags" began to understand the truth. Miriam had opened the door for him. He went off on a long walk, eventually putting down his bags, feeling very tired, and wanting to rest. "Money bags" noticed a beautiful building glowing in many colours and felt compelled to walk through the gate and walked up a beautiful path with all the glorious flowers and trees. He was met and taken into a beautiful room filled with flowers and a couch, being told to rest and sleep as long as he wished. After the rest, he came to speak with us again. Having had a long sleep, being very tired from continually protecting his money. On awakening, his money bags were brought to him, but he realized the truth and no longer desired them.,

Now he has told us that his real name is Arthur, that his Guide had always been with him and that he had seen him following all the time, also that he had not listened to him, thinking he was after his money and also not realising that he was his Guardian Angel.

Arthur said that now he is a very rich man, no one can take away what he has learned and now knows the power of positive' thinking, and will use it to good advantage.

Arthur still likes to wonder over the hills and lovely valleys, enjoying the great beauty of the Spirit World. Arthur also decided that he was ready to help those Souls who come over into the Spirit World in a similar condition. He will always remember that love is the foundation of the Spirit Life, a purified life.

Keep the love of Father God with you, the most precious jewel of all is the love of God. Arthur realised Jesus was a poor man who wanted for nothing.

FIVE

BENJAMIN

This is a story of a young boy in his teens and what happened to him. Benjamin and some friends went out one evening to have a good time. The evening ended in a terrible car crash, with no knowledge of how it had happened, ending up with one of his arms completely severed. The Doctor found the remaining arm so badly damaged that it had to be removed. In this condition and in a great sense of shock, he lingered for three days, having thoughts that he could not survive with his body this way, pleased when he lost consciousness, for he was convinced that he was permanently without arms.

Benjamin had never followed any religion or ever prayed during his lifetime, thinking he had no need of the Father God, thinking the Father could do nothing for him, he had to fight his own battles in life. So he passed into the Spirit World with these thoughts.

Benjamin knew that he had passed into Spirit, but would not accept the help brought by his Guide, telling him that everything can be restored in Spirit. Benjamin could only believe what he saw. If he could not see his arms, how could he imagine that they were there? It is ridiculous, how can I have Spirit arms?

Benjamin's Guide told him, "you never thought you could speak to people in Spirit either, did you?" No, he had never given it a thought. He was asked to build a perfect picture of himself in his mind, as he used to be before the accident, whilst a prayer was said, bringing healing and restoring perfection to his mind.

One leaves the worn out earthly body behind at the time of passing into the Spirit World, the Spirit body at the time of passing being perfect, the Christ Spirit in all is perfect; imperfections are only in the mind.

Through the power during the prayer, Benjamin opened his eyes at the end to eventually accept that his arms and hands were in perfect working order. On leaving, he told us he was going to pray himself and give thanks to Father God for his wonderful miracle.

SIX

THE HANGMAN

The minds of Souls passed into the Spirit World continue to be tormented by the life style they followed on the earth plane and continue to be very unhappy.

In this story, the Soul concerned had been a hangman during his life span. This Soul came through our Rescue Circle in great distress, convinced he could never gain forgiveness from the Father God, as his commandment is "Thou salt not kill."

He was haunted by many Souls around him who were crying for mercy, making his life an absolute misery. His thoughts were, "what I have done, I can never undo," feeling he must live for ever condemned. Condemned by his own mind, his own consciousness, not by the Father God, who only sees perfection in his children. He said, he must condemn himself, cannot forgive himself, what he had done was unforgiveable. "How can I find peace? I have been to many sanctuaries, but cannot find peace. I have to find peace, I cannot forgive myself for the dreadful things I have done all my life. My Soul cannot rest in peace, I can't, I can't." Then he cried "Forgive me, forgive me."

A prayer was said, asking Father God to grant peace, forgiveness and a blessing. When a Soul asks for our Father God's help, the response is immediate.

On the realisation that he had been granted peace, he went to rest and in time met those who had been his victims, to find that they had forgiven him. He became a channel for the Father's work helping many troubled Souls.

He has helped many Souls who pass into the Spirit World in similar conditions and who had passed death sentences on many people. These Souls had also suffered much agonising mental torment for maybe many years of our earthly time, they too eventually discovered their victims had forgiven them and that they were not condemned by them.

SEVEN

ONE OF MY LIVES - JONATHAN

This story was related to us, many incarnations after it was experienced, by Jonathan, now a highly evolved spirit, having gone through many different incarnations, living through all types of conditions of life, learning many lessons in striving to develop perfection.
This is chosen to show the difference of your life now and a severing of the life into the Spirit.
Life as a young man and growing up in an extremely strict family, the law being, the law of the belt. With no half measures; once his father started, he often forgot to stop.
In his own words; I was about 15 years of age, and had a great fondness for animals, my great desire being to own, love and bring up a dog. My father said they were useless, treacherous and unfaithful. A very old friend, a very old man, knew of this and said he would get a dog and keep it there with him. I could come over and feed it, wash it, brush it and look after it. My father was not to know.
Of course, I thought this a wonderfully grand idea. Within myself I had a great fear of my father, always seeing him with horns sticking out of his head. He represented the devil in every way, never a kind word, never a request - always a command; do it or else. One can hardly imagine such a man could exist now, but it was very much so at the time.
I had to do a certain amount of work at home on my knees, not to pray, I did not know how, but to scrub floors and clean, etc. My mother was a gentle soul and tried to smooth things out, also getting into hot water at times. Father was very harsh with my mother.
My friend obtained a beautiful little puppy, a collie type dog. This wonderful old man, and I certainly love him, taught me how to look after my new wonderful friend. All went well for about a year and then my father got to know that I had a dog, because I was not always at home and father wanted to know where I was going all the time.

I told my father that I went to a friend's house when my work was finished, as they needed help. He did not believe me, and followed me one day and saw me with my dog. He had a very thick belt with a very thick buckle. I always thought that if I could get hold of the belt, he would not see it again, but suppose he'd get hold of something else far worse Nevertheless, he got hold of me and thrased me, he then thrashed the dog until he killed it.

Well just imagine my state of mind. These are parts of my life I do not like to recall, for it was only a year after that, that I passed into Spirit. Partly through my father's treatment and partly through the fear that had grown in me, slowly it had killed me. It had eaten into me like a disease. I was afraid to go home if I was out and it naturally ate into me. In time I became sick, father even refused to get a doctor, said I was just shamming to get out of work. My mother called a doctor but it was too late. I passed into the Spirit World with congested lungs through the beatings I had had on my back.

With all the years of fear, my mind was in a terrible state when I passed into Spirit. The last thing I saw was my poor mother, old and broken hearted, because she knew I should have lived into manhood. as I closed my eyes and darkness came, I saw a hideous apparition laughing at me, saying you are coming with me; I was petrified. I had a powerful Egyptian Guide, but who was powerless at this time, because it was the state of my mind which had built up this apparition.

The Guide just oozed out love, but my mind was so poisoned, I just went through a darkness that was so black and heavy and could feel it weighing me down. I did not see my Guide although he never left me, Guides never do, no matter what your condition. I just went on travelling through darkness, aware of voices laughing or a word here and there. I continued on like this, until suddenly, I thought to myself, why should I go through this sort of thing, I had had enough in the past. I will get away from all this. I will not accept it.

At that very moment there was a flash of light, my Guide stood in front of me, and said "My son it shall be so." He took my hand, he was filled with so much warmth and love and reaslised that he was taking me through beautiful corridors, illuminated by different colours. Colours that were alive and glimmering. I could feel the welcome. The doors were studded with light, like diamonds, which opened before we reached them, into a beautiful hall. Upon entering this beautiful hall,

there was complete silence, a beautiful silence. I was led to a couch, to relax and find peace and to clear my mind completely.
The colours were completely overshadowing me, each colour bringing even balance to all parts of the body, building up the Spirit, which you are.
After a period of rest, my Guide took me to a room filled with beautiful flowers. I had not worried much about flowers, these were magnificient, the colour pink, which is for love. The love I had missed. I lay down on a couch of pink flowers and slept. my Guide was there when I awakened, having sat with me all the time.
Later I met my old friend and my beautiful dog. After a long time in Spirit and when I had a better understanding, I met my father. He who had been so masterful and determined, was now a very humble person. After a touching reunion, father also asked my forgiveness and I said there was nothing to forgive that had happened in another world.
All must eliminate fear, it is a mental poisoning that eats Into you. In place of fear, place *THE FATHER* within, be strengthened, and built up in the Christ Spirit, have *no fear*. When you have understanding, accepting the Father's teachings, you will awaken in a beautiful Spirit World, of unexpressable beauty.

EIGHT

JUDGE NOT

So much soul searching faces a judge in this earthly profession, but apparently an even greater mental torment faces them when returning to the real world, the world of the Spirit; The Father's Kingdom.
They have been unable to observe the Father's commandment "Thou shalt not kill," during their life's work. They do indeed judge themselves and are filled with regret, concern and condemnation of their own judgement on those brought before them.
One to tell us his story is Judge McCarthy. His job to condemn man for the sins he committed. But he was in no way perturbed over it, certainly he did not lose any sleep, or have any sense of pity; it was his job. There were times (but not often) that he felt a little restless inside, when having to pronounce the death sentence on a youth. His seniors demanded justice, that punishment must be metted out to those who deserved it, it was a form of protection for wives and daughters who had been criminally assaulted.
He was married, and had three sons and two daughters. If a son of his had committed a deed that deserved punishment, as a father, he would have felt the same as any other human being, but justice would have to be carried out. He felt what right had he to say to a man, "You shall hang by the neck until you are dead, may God have mercy on.your Soul." Justice was a life for a life, an eye for an eye.
During one of his court sessions, he suffered a heart attack and landed in the Spirit World. It was then that he saw life from a completely different view. He saw the agony, the tortured minds, the collapse of courage when condemned to die. He knows only one thing, he is cut off from the world. When he enters Spirit, he is a demented Soul, with all the accumulation of fear going through the emotion of hell, a Soul wandering in darkness.
Judge McCarthy was also tormented by what he had had to do, and

eventually was only consoled when able to meet some of the condemned Souls; who had found peace and were willing to forgive him and bear him no malice.

The Judge now spiritually adjusted, has dedicated himself to helping every condemned Soul that comes over. This work he has chosen to clear his Soul, that which he sustained doing is the very thing he now condemns.

NINE

FEAR OF DEATH (CHILDREN)

The first thing to irradicate is the fear of death. There are millions of Souls constantly passing into the Spirit World in fear and darkness (darkness being a state of mind) when, with the right thoughts, they could enjoy peace and light. The older people perhaps in pain and longing for death, yet still in fear, not knowing what happens when death comes and that when so-called death comes, that their pain will go; so they are going into God's Kingdom completely distraught.

What to tell a child who will ask "What is it like to die?" The usual answer is, "Oh! you go to heaven, you go to God," and they have no idea just what is meant by heaven.

These children go over looking for heaven, looking for God; bewildered when unable to find him. All children believe in fairy stories, so when a child asks the question about death, it would be good to ask "what would you like most in the world?"

Describe heaven as being like fairyland, where there is no pain or sickness, nothing to be frightened of, but that it is so beautiful. Here you can have all the pets you want, as all the animals are tame and all love to be stroked. You can make friends with them all. There are other children to play with of all ages, in such beautiful gardens where you can have just whatever you would like. Even the house made of ginger bread, wlth windows made of chocolate. All the lovely things children dream about. They can have whatever they want. Also that they wlll never be parted from their parents, for even though their parents may still be on the earth plane, during the time when the parents are sleeping at night, they will be re-united and will be able to show them around and, in this way, never losing touch. There is so much love, joy and happiness. They will see fairies alive and flying around, singing, and will hear the lovely soft music.

As the moment comes when they close their eyes to this world, they are re-united with loved ones and enter this beautiful summerland. There are mountains to climb, seas to play in, there are no storms, no cold, no hot sun, just perfect beauty. The only learning is learning the love of Jesus.

TEN

WHAT OF THE ELDERLY?

If only the fear was taken out of dying; they would have no problems. Only a mere handful of all those who pass into the Spirit World have the knowledge of the life awaiting them.
The earth at present is filled with disaster areas, terrible accidents, hate and war, all kinds of terror and fear. So many lives on earth come to a fearful and abrupt end, returning to God's Kingdom with minds in terrible conflict and pain and in need of love and peace.
These Souls can only be reached by prayer, for so many will not listen or accept when informed about the real life in Spirit when on earth, so they cannot accept help from their Guides (their Guardian Angels) after passing; not even accepting that they have died and left the earth plane; so they remain in torment.
How simple and peaceful life can be when one has already accepted the teachings before passing into Spirit.
I will relate the description of the transition from this earth, as told to us by a lady who lived close to us, and had no fear of so called dying. Her name was Dulcie, and in her own words this was her experience.

ELEVEN

DULCIE

I felt I would like to come to explain to all my friends in detail what it is like to (what they so-call) 'die.'
Be assured that with understanding, your loved ones are always with you, there is absolutely no division, as love binds you together. One moment I was lying in my hospital bed, and the very next I opened my eyes (of course my third eye) and there was my husband, who had passed over many years before and my Guide. Just as simple as that, like waking in the morning.
I remember so vividly the excitement of meeting my husband, Morris. I put my hand out to him and the other out to my Guide, who is Chinese. Although conscious that I was in a hospital room, all pain and discomfort had gone. I was free of pain and I could see again. As they lifted me up, I said I would like to go to see my little dogs. They agreed, it is always your last wish that is of utmost importance to your Guide. I closed my eyes, just letting myself go with them and instantaneously I was with my dogs. They knew me, so I sat playing with them for a few minutes of your earth time. I gave a blessing to my children and a prayer that they would be looked after. With my Guide and my husbands arm around me, we just seemed to float and rise hiqher and higher. The higher we were, the lighter I felt.
During this transition, I felt the power of love from my loved ones. So wrapped up in this joy of being with Morris, I was only conscious of this wonderful love and peace, the joy of going up. When we reached the first plane, where all must go, there were my loved ones in the garden, near the sanitorium. You are allowed to speak with your loved ones, my parents and relatives without being rushed. Eventually, we separated and I went on to the sanitorium.
At the gardens of the sanitorium, there were beautiful steps that seemed to vibrate in many built in colours. There is such a beautiful fountain,

with the sounds of tinkling music coming from the water as it fell into the pool below.
I was led along a corridor of flowers, and the perfume is unbelievable that emanates from the flowers. I was led to a beautiful couch covered in flowers and, by this time, I was ready and happy to lie down. Then I remembered that I should go to Padre's Chapel to thank the Father God, so asked my Guide to take me. Padre was one of the brothers of Jesus; the Chapel was small, but filled with the power of love and peace. The gentleness, kindness and love of Padre was present, and he wished me God's Blessings, saying how pleased he was I had remembered to thank the Father. I returned to my flowered bed, lay down, and slept the most perfect sleep I had experienced in many years.
The time came, I awakened and my Guide was there. I felt I had absorbed so much peace and I now wanted to get up. He agreed, as there was so much I wlshed to see. You cannot just walk through a Spirit garden as you would on earth. There is so much merging of yourself in the beauty and sound. Every flower seems to have its own sound and tune. When my Guide thought I had reached the stage where I was ready, I went out of the garden, back to my loved ones. Back to my husband and a beautiful garden, a place which he had prepared for me. In this peace, this stillness and the timelessness of everything, I began to think about my friends and loved ones who had passed into the Spirit Kingdom before me.
As for loved ones left behind in different parts of the country on the earth plane, by my thought I am instantaneously with them and I hear them say, "I know Dulcie is here," some will say "I feel Dulcie."
I have laughed so much since being here, discussing the silly faults and fears we had on earth. One thing I must emphasize, there is no such thing as dying. You are alive every split second of your life, it is as simple as that.

TWELVE

RETURN TO SPIRIT OF LOVED ONE

One occasion which all must experience during the life span on earth, is the return of a loved one to their true Spiritual home. One which could be made less dramatic and sad if considered in this light.
There are times when a friend or loved one may leave their beautiful home and come to visit for a period. You are sharing joys, sorrows, fun and happiness, drawing you closer together. They are only with you for a limited time and must return home; when there may be tears of farewell.
You have done so much together and are sorry to see them go. But you know they are returning home. Your thoughts and love go with them, "God be with you," as you travel back to a distant land; knowing that as they return they are met by other loved ones, who will welcome them. Although you feel sadness when a loved one has passed into Spirit, and wish they were back with you, you know they will spend the rest of their time where they belong, in their true home. You will not write sorrowful letters, begging them to return, you wish them well. This is as it should be, when a loved one returns to their Spiritual home. They have been sent to you for a short time, to bring joy and love and help you make spiritual progress, but must return. So you say farewell, sending out a light of love. All sorrow will be wiped away, for you know no matter what happens, you will meet again in Spirit. Where you are linked in true love, you will meet again in another incarnation; you will never lose the ones you love. With this understanding, you will find comfort and peace. Let there be no sadness, only lovely memories, beautiful thoughts of all you have shared. God be with you till we meet again.

THIRTEEN

I HAVE FOUND PEACE
CAMELIA GRANT

Good evening. Please, I am a little nervous. You see, I have found that I am not as wonderful as I thought I was.

My name is Camelia Grant and when I was on the earth plane I worked in a very big business. I had a responsible position and I felt grand. It felt wonderful to think that, without me, the business could not be possibly work right. I had so much in this business. I felt so much above everyone else. You could say, I was the boss. My word carried a great deal of weight. To me it was everything.

This business played a great part in my life and, as I grew older, I grew more self confident. I grew with the years very big and very high. I found myself extremely alone. I had no family. I had not married. Why should I? I was capable of looking after myself.

Then someone, whom I presume felt sorry for me, why, I don t know, for I was a most capable person, came to me and asked me if I was happy. at that time I thought; "What a ridiculous question." Of course I was happy, I had everything; controlled a business, but they persisted that I was not happy. I said; "How mistaken you are. I am completely happy. I want for nothing, absolutely nothing." They said to me; "You may have everything you want, but there is one precious thing you do not possess." I said; "What would that be?" They said; "You haven't God". I said; "GOD? What has He got to do with it? He has nothing to do with my work. He has nothing to do with the way I have worked myself up to the position I have this day. Why do you have to bring that to me?" They said; "Because, while you may have the credit of working yourself up to this position, you have not the love of The Father within you." I said; "I don't require it. I am capable and I shall continue to be capable. What else do I need?"

I was so stubborn. I was so selfish. I was the only one alive! But there came the day that I fell ill. Of course, I did not pray. Why should I? The doctor said to me; " I must speak to you and tell you the truth. You will never get up from this bed again." I did not believe him. I said; "But this is nonsense, I am quite capable of getting up from this bed when I feel better." He shook his head and I asked; "Do you mean to tell me that I am not going to get better? I am going to die?" The Doctor turned away and walked out of the room.

I can't tell you, I can't express in words what I felt. I felt the loss of everything. I thought; "What are they going to do without me?" Then a voice said; "You cannot expect to go on for ever and ever." I said; "No, I realise that, but not now."

Then came a darkness, so dark I could not see a thing. For a moment I thought I was blind. I was blind, blind to the truth. Then I felt I was not stationary, I was moving, but I was moving in darkness and I thought; "Perhaps the light is not here, but where is the window?" I felt so light. I felt I had no weight in me. Suddenly, the darkness cleared and I saw myself amongst people and yet not amongst them. They walked past me. They were strangers and they were friends, friends that I had known through business contacts and I spoke to them but they did not hear me. They did not see me.

I was bewildered. I saw my mother and I thought; "Oh, thank goodness, I have found my mother. At least she will know me." I went to her. She did not see me, so I walked away from everyone until I came to a bare piece of ground that looked as though it never had a flower or a tree or a blade of grass on it. I stopped and thought; "What has happened to me? Where am I?" and a voice said to me; "You are as you have always been, alone."

"What does it feel like now that you seek companionship, now that you seek recognition and you find that no one sees you? What does it feel like?"

I started to cry and turned to the voice. I could not see where it came from but I said; "Where am I? This is so strange." The voice said; "You are in spirit." So I said; "I died. I did die," and the reply was "No, you are not dead. You are very much alive." I said; "What must I do?" and the voice said: "Seek the Father in all His Love and Glory." And you know, strangely enough, the very sound of that name went like a shock through me. I said; "No, I don't want to meet Him."

I was still arrogant. I still did not want to know the truth. Was I afraid of it? Perhaps I was and he said to me; (for it was a man's voice) "My child, if you do not seek you will never find Him and you will walk, and continue to walk, alone in this spiritual world until you find the Love which the Father has offered to you. Come with me." and I followed this voice. He took me to a beautiful hall and said; "Relax."

There was a couch in this hall. It was not a very big hall, and it was very beautiful, such lovely colours which seemed as though they were a live. He said; "Now relax." I lay on this couch and relaxed as I thought. Then I said; "Are you still here?" and he replied: "I am still here with you." "Where am I?" and he said; "You are in the Hall of Memory."

As I lay there and permitted my mind to relax, the memories of the past crowded on to me, so fast, so true' I saw myself as others had seen me and I realised that I was not one of them. I was not a part of them, I couldn t be because I, myself, had broken away from them. and, as the memories crowded through in vivid pictures, I saw my life as I had lived it. Then I saw a beautiful light which seemed to shine down upon me from nowhere, for there was no window, but this light came, so white, so bright, so much warmth, and I cried; "are you still there?" I did not know his name, he said ; "Yes, my child, I am still here."

I said; "Tell me, where does this light come from and what is it?" He said; "This is the Love of the Father and it pours into you. The Father is within all His children. The Father has been within you and you have tried to crush Him. The Spirit can never be crushed nor broken, for Spirit is eternal life." I said; "Take me to Him." But he said; "No, I do not take you to Him neither does He come to you. You shall find Him in your way, the way of Spirit, the way which the Father has taught all His children; Come unto me and I will give you rest.'"

"You will find more realisation of the truth of the Love of God as you continue in your progress. You are now within His home. You are bathed with the Light of His Love. Seek Him whenever you desire and He will answer you call."

He then took me to a beautiful room, yet it was not a room. It was filled with flowers, it had beautiful arched windows to it and the vibration, that I learned afterwards was not the atmosphere, was so beautiful, so peaceful. I said to the voice; "I am tired." He said; "It should be so. Now you will rest and you will sleep for a while."

I do not know how long I slept, but I have now been awake a long time. I have completely changed my thoughts and my ways of living, and I try

always to go forward to help others. *I have found peace.* I have not yet found the Father, not as I want to find Him, but I will, I surely will for I have learnt to love the very Name that brings so much power and so much happiness and upliftment to so many.
May this love, may this beautiful light, that shone on me, shine upon you all, that you, too, might find what I found, the complete release of an earthly life, a life that is burdened, a life that is controlled only by your own thoughts and, before I go, may I ask you to take the Father with you in everything you do and in every thought that you think. Take Him into your confidence. Take your troubles to Him and be completely confident and He will help you. So I ask that His blessing may abide with you all for I feel that I would love to come back to this earth. Perhaps He will permit me to do so one day, so that I might bring the teachings, the teachings that I will have by then.

FOURTEEN

LADY AGATHA

Good evening. I was known during my life time as Lady Agatha and I met Lady Norah.

I was an old woman when I came into Spirit, not knowing anything, but still very conscious of my standing as Lady Agatha. I belonged to what is known as the aristocracy and did not know what a childhood was like as you see your children play today.

We were stiffly brought up, never allowed to be untidy nor to romp. It was unladylike. We used to have boots that buttoned up to the knees and long sleeves. All so very prim and proper and that is how I grew up, very straightlaced, starched you might say.

No one dared speak to Lady Agatha unless I spoke first, so conscious of one's standing, so conscious of what was correct. I have seen your life today and you don't know how lucky you are, particularly your children. We were confined in a playroom. Every minute of our day was set for something. In the snow we had to walk like a lady. We could lever let go. We could never laugh out loudly. It was common to laugh. I never married, so I did not know the joys of having children. I was a starched, severe old spinster.

Then I came into Spirit, and I remember very clearly when gave my name out as Lady Agatha, Norah said; "I am Lady Norah," and the others laughed and I was very tempted to laugh, but I was afraid they might be poking fun at me. It would not do to laugh. So when she asked me if I would like to see my guide, a little girl arrived.

I could not believe that I could possibly have a child as a guide. I was not very happy. I did not know how to take this child, pretty little girl. She still is and it was only when Bill said to me "Didn't Jesus say; 'and a little child shall lead them'?" I thought well, yes, and so I left with this child, a little chatterbox, joyous and so full of love and laughter, sunshine and happiness, and I went along this pathway with beautiful trees on either side. This little chatterbox pranced around at my side pointing out the different houses and buildings, showing me where everything was.

Then she took me up to the Rest Home, this lovely place, more magnificient than I have ever seen a building before, and as I walked up those steps, this little thing running up the steps, trying to hurry me on, but I was still Lady agatha. Then we went inside and she showed me where I would rest, that little voice prattling along, and I really did not know how I was going to cope with this. So I had my rest.

Then she said, "come along, I want to show you all the things that I know are pretty," and she did too. She showed me the simple, pretty little things. I went down on my knees to see the tiny little flowers in the grass with many little snails and caterpillars. She showed me the beauty of them. She taught me so much of the insect life which I had never experienced on the earth plane. She sang songs and took me to the birds. At times I thought poor little thing, she must think I am a load to carry, but gradually I began to relax and to laugh with her and to see the beauty of all that is in the Spirit World She had many tiny little creatures, birds and kittens. She took me to the water. She laughed, rolling over in delight when I walked through the little stream and was amazed that my feet did not get wet, and then she showed me how to walk by thought. By this time, I had learned to laugh too and she would take my hand and we would float and this became a great game to her. We weren't the only ones doing this. It is a marvellous sensation. There were all types of people experimenting with this new way of walking and when she felt that I had been able to overcome the novelty of seeing her, her little life, she began to take me to more adult things.

I listened to all with a childish mind and ear. I went to different buildings and I saw dancing. I heard music, and with much laughter and joy, I too, rode the elephants and lions, and I can only say if anyone ever receives a child for a guide, they do not realise what a wonderful gift they will have been given, for within that childish body is, of course, an adult mind.

In everything that we did, I lost my starchiness. I became a child. All that I had missed on the earth plane, I found. I enjoyed everything, and my Guide takes me to all these places, even to what is known as the lecture rooms. I listened to some of those lectures, I thought this little thing could not possibly understand, but she sat there and we discussed the talks after we left. It was like having a child of my own, a joy that I had never experienced. From her, I learnt to laugh and sing. We went everywhere and all the time she was showing me the way of life in Spirit. Eventually, she, too, told me that I will see the picture of my life. I have not reached that stage yet, but I will do. With her beside me I shall not be worried for I am quite sure that she will become almost hysterical at all the things which I did.

So, be happy, be happy with your guide. The experience of having that one with you is wonderful. I am so happy and hope never again will I ever miss out on so much that there is to enjoy on the earth plane. So I will leave you now and I am very happy that I have been able to come through and speak to you. The peace and love are well worth waiting for.

FIFTEEN

REGINALD - A TORMENTED MIND

I greet you all. I come as a very humble man. My name is Reginald. As you were told, I came as a rescue case because when I went into Spirit, all I could see around me were the eyes of the animals that I had shot. I will not distress you by going into details, for I know that not one of you has ever lived the life that I did.

I was an army man, proud, obstinate and a very difficult man, for I expected all my orders that I gave to my men and to my servant to be given first priority in all that they did. As far as I was concerned, no one had a private life, and my life and my love was shooting. I prided myself on my markmanship and like everyone else who attains perfection in something or other, they are looked up to. They are paid homage, even if it be hunting, it is done in sport. It is done in every walk of life. If you are outstanding, you are a big man, and so it was when I was posted to India as a Colonel of a Regiment, I was given my first taste of shooting animals, and if I could excuse myself by saying that I shot to feed the hungry or to save someone. I can't. I shot for the glory of killing.

I wanted to be looked up to. I did not want people to think, particularly the Indians and the Black Men (I also went to Africa) that I was a coward, so every animal I wanted, I would go and seek. I did not do the work, it was these unfortunate Black Men, who I realise now are my brothers in Christ in the Father, and when they had tracked down the animals, so I rode along in my glory on elephants, and shot them. I shot them for trophies So that I could say I had more than the others. I could claim fame to more killings than any other man.

If only I had realised what I was doing. What I had done and what I have done. It still makes me sick at heart, for I think it is one of the most useless, cruel and wicked sports there is, for these poor unfortunate animals had no way of defending themselves, yet, I gloried in it, and all I ask now is for the opportunity that I might come back to this earth again and fight for all these animals against all the cruelty that is still taking place on your earth plane.

I have been shown the very animals that I shot, for they are here in the Spirit World. There was no hatred in their looks, no fear. There was love, and as I walk around them now, I feel as though I am what you might call a pint-size. I glory in their beauty, and I have to make retribution somehow for I will have to find this peace and the only way I can do it now is to try to impress all those upon your earth plane who are still perpetrating these acts of cruelty and wickedness upon the animals today and beseech that you make yourself felt to bring power to any organization that is trying to put a stop to cruelty, even in the cause of medicine, which cannot benefit.

As those who eat meat have been told, the fear of the animals, the vibrations of fear remain in the flesh, therefore, does not the fear vibration remain in the medicines that are made from animals, those tortured, killed? Yes, I have been shown during my short time while in Spirit, that these animals killed and tortured, are used in the beauty preparations for women, no wonder these is so much unhappiness in your world today.

If you see a tiny bird in difficulties, help it. Even the tiniest of animals created in the peferfection of the Father's love, the glory of the big animals, those that are now extinct throught the cruelty of man, I ask you to pray for them, pray for all those in Spirit who are doing rescue work, that I too, may join this band or that I may one day return to this earth plane to undo some of the hurt and harm that I have already done.

In this Chapel, as I sit here, is a peace which I have never known before. Where in your world do you find this love and this peace? How fortunate you are, how truly blessed you are, and I have seen and been shown the light as it shines out from your prayers, in such brilliance, radiating far beyond your imagination.

Let this light go out to all those misguided men, such as was, and to all those misguided doctors and scientists and pray that the Spirit, the Soul of those that are tortured will find peace and pure love from those in Spirit, when they reach it.

I thank you for listening for I feel so humble. I never realised that a man could feel so humble, yet so good and so at peace. Bless you for this light and the prayers and love that you radiate to all.

SIXTEEN

"FINDING OF PEACE"
by Chuck

I cannot stay long as I have been listening to this talk about peace. You may call me Chuck and when I was on the earth plane as you call it, that was one thing I never thought of and did not want, I did not want stillness and silence; you have the likes of me all over your earth plane today where all we want is noise, loud music, revving up our bikes. Mom used to ask me to sit quietly and speak to her and I used to say I did not want to be quiet. We had our guitars and the louder they went the more we like it, and as we strummed I know we made people angry, we got on their nerves for they wanted peace and guiet and we did not; this is how I went through my life, anything for noise, must be on the move and I was on my motor bike revving it up.

Suddenly everything was dead still, I did not know what had happened. I wandered around and I could see people walking. I could see motor cars but I could not hear anything. I thought I had gone deaf, so I went along to the place where I knew the gang had their guitars, still I could not hear a thing, I called to the gang that they were not playing loudly enough, but they took no notice of me. Then I got frightened and I do not know whether I prayed, I cannot remember, but someone came up to me and spoke, he asked me "Are you lost?" I said "No, I thought I was deaf but I can hear you speaking." "No, you are not deaf, you were very careless. On the motor bike you were making so much noise you did not hear or see the bus in front of you." I said, "I have pranged and I have had it?" He said; "Yes," I said I did not mind but I wanted noise, I wanted to hear noise I could not take this stillness; so he said "Come with me." I followed him and he took me to a place where there was an orchestra such as I knew, it was making all the noise I wanted and I was happy.

Then he told me to come a little further away and I said I did not want to go into the quiet but he said I would hear the music. So we walked quite far and I did hear the music but not as loud as it was when I was close to them. He took me to a garden and I could still hear faint music and there was so much beauty in the garden but after a while I began to call out that I wanted music, I wanted noise, I could not take the silence, so I asked him to take me back to this orchestra and after some time, he would say come, and we would walk away and I would go back to this beautiful garden and this happened many times; many times I went back to the loud music until eventually felt I could not take the noise of the music anymore and called out for help.

I found myself sitting on a bench in the lovely garden and there was a most beautiful little bird who came and sat on a branch of a tree. I do not know the names of flowers or birds, and this tree was full of flowers and this little bird began to sing and I thought if I could pick that tune up on my guitar, it would be something beautiful and my attention was drawn to that little bird; then a few more birds came and they started their songs; songs that you have never heard before. Then I realised that I was hearing the noise from the orchestra and I wanted it to stop, as I was engrossed in listening to these little birds, so I called out "stop that music," and it stopped. Then this man asked my why I stopped the music and I said it was drowning the song of these little birds and I could only hear them when it was quiet. He said "You have learnt your lesson You can only hear beauty when there is quiet and stillness and I will take you to another place where it is even more quiet." There were no birds and he told me to listen to the music in the grass, the trees and, as I listened, I was filled with something I had never experienced in my whole life. He told me that I had discovered the peace that comes when you can sit by yourself.

That was my beginning of realising that in this stillness you can hear voices, you can hear music, you can hear birds. I have yet to go and sleep, they have told me to do so now because the material vibrations have been worn away and I am already thinking of a way to try to bring this knowledge, this experience to others, but this must wait until I have had my sleep. I have seen where I am going to sleep, it is the most beautiful place, and I have only seen beauty ever since I have been here, I am looking forward to the quiet and the stillness and I can only ask if perhaps some of you who may know some youngsters like I was, try to help them.

SEVENTEEN

THE STORY OF REUBEN

In a quiet little village there was a small boy called Reuben, and this little one was a holy terror. He fought with all the little pets and the birds and whatever he could do that was not right, he surely did it.

He was feared by the children of this village for they were a peaceful and a loving community. Actually, they were shepherds and when the shepherds saw Reuben coming along, they gathered their sheep together.

One day Reuben came across a shepherd and his flock and although this man knew Reuben, he was not frightened of him. Reuben greeted him; "Hello shep." To which the shephered replied; "Hello, Reuben, what do you think you are going to do today?" "Oh," he said, "I don't know. I have not thought about it yet." The shepherd said; "How can you go around with an empty mind like that, just not thinking? Don't you think it would be very nice to sit down and have a chat with someone, have a talk with me? I am sure we have a lot in common to discuss."

Reuben kicked some stones and thought. "Well," he said; "Maybe." The shepherd said; "There is a nice tree over there. Let us go and sit and relax." They marched over to the tree and sat in the shade to relax. The shepherd said to him; "Reuben, first of all, tell me one thing. What do you mostly think about? What is the one thought in your mind?" Reuben replied; "Oh shep, I don't know, my mind is filled with a lot of things and they all come like this and that and I could not say which one of them I think mostly of."

"Supposing you relax now and try to think which of those confusing thoughts is the most predominant." "Actually," Reuben said, "Every time I try to concentrate on one thought, that thought is that I would love to know that people and the animals are all scared of me." The shepherd said; "Really?" "Yes," came the reply, "You know there is nobody who can fight me." The shepherd said; "Don't be too sure about that because one day someone will teach you very severe lessons." "Oh that is an old story. That is what my mother is always telling me and I don't believe it. So far I have been the victor. I am the one who always comes out tops." The shepherd said; "Well, that might be so at the moment, but do you really feel good inside to see dogs and cats and little children run away from you?" Reuben answered; "Sure I do, why not? I won't allow anybody to kick me around."

The shepherd replied; "You are only a little boy now, but if you keep this up through life, what do you expect to get in the end? You will have no friends. No one will respect you. No one who will want to come to you and ask you advice. Don't you think it is nice if someone has enough confidence in you to come to you and say, Reuben, I am in trouble. Please help me out. Tell me what to do. Show me what to do. Don't you think, Reuben, that that is a very nice way of living? To be able to help some one who cannot be helped by others and instead of them being afraid of you, they will seek you out and come to you, not only one, but perhaps in crowds. The animals will come to you to be petted and you will still be master of the situation."

Reuben did not like that very much and said; "I think that is being weak." "Oh no, you heard the story of Jesus and you know how they threw stones at Him, how they spat at Him, how that tortured Him and yet was He not Master of that situation because He was far above it? It mattered not what they did, He still walked with His head high, and His step was firm. There are many ways of being the Master of a situation under any condition and in each and every way there is the right way which brings the better result. There is no fun, there is no honour to have the kind of mastery that will bring fear."

Reuben said; "Oh shep, I don't think I am in the mood to talk today" "Alright, Reuben," said the shepherd, "If you are a little tired, I will leave you and tend my flock." He got up very gently and went away.

After a little while Reuben got up, put his hands in hls pockets and kicked the stones as he walked along. He was really in a very bad mood. Why did the shepherd talk to him like that? Why did he have to disturb him inside? Now he cannot make up his mind what he wants to be. He will not go near him anymore.

This train of thought kept on and on until he reached the foot of the hills and there he saw a rabbit, a pure white rabbit caught in a trap. Ordinarily, Reuben would have stoned it. But he passed it. He looked at it and thought; "Well, it serves you right. You don't look where you are going." He walked on a few steps, but he turned back and thought; "The poor thing must be in pain." So he got a thick stick to prise open this trap and released the rabbit.

The rabbit was covered in blood and its paw was broken. He picked it up and went back to the shepherd who asked him; "What have you got there?" Reuben explained that it was a rabbit which had been caught in a snare. "Oh, what a pity," the shepherd said "Don't you think we had better kill it?" Reuben looked at him but the shepherd continued; "You know it is in terrible pain and I think it is better that we kill it" Reuben objected; "No, no shep, you know what I am going to do? I am going to take this rabbit home and I will cure it. I will make it better." The shepherd patted him on his shoulder and said; "Good boy, you go and make the rabbit better."

He took the rabbit home and said to his mother; "I am going to make this rabbit better and it is going to be my pet." His mother looked at him in disbelief and said; "Are you feeling right, my child?" "Of course I am alright. Why?" "No", she said, "I just wondered. How will you make it better?" "I am going to bathe it and clean the wound and bandage it." This he did and after about a week the rabbit started to respond and although it could not walk or hop properly, it was no more in pain and followed Reuben everywhere. Everybody used to say; "Here comes Reuben and his rabbit." It followed him down to the place where the shepherd tended his sheep. The shepherd greeted him with; "Well, Reuben, I never thought it of you." "What do you mean, you never thought it of me?" Reuben asked. "You remember the little talk we had and you said that you liked to be the master of a situation?" Reuben replied; "Yes," and the shepherd continued; "Don't you think you have become the supreme master of that situation? You have permitted that little rabbit to live and on top of that to help it with its paw and make it better and above all those things, to keep it to love."

Reuben looked at the rabbit and then back at the shepherd. "You know, shep, I thought you were kidding me with something. I will go down into that valley and I am going to try and find out where I can be the master of every situation where help is needed."

He walked away from the shepherd, but just before he went down into the dip towards the valley, he turned and waved his hand to the shephered and as he did this, the shephered had a beautiful Light around him and he had a beard. He was transfigured into the likeness of Christ.

Reuben looked, turned round and walked down into the valley. He knew then and there that he had been talking to the Spirit, the Christ Spirit within, the shepherd, and it made him feel good. It made him feel whole and it made him feel that he was really wanted.

As he grew up into manhood, he visited many, many homes and gave much help in healing and prayers and also dressing of wounds and cleansing of sores, because he now realised that he was doing the work of Christ.

Perhaps it is good to remember the story of Reuben. To remember it that it might be given to someone who has the tendency to be master of a situation, so masterful that it causes hurts and fear, to be turned into a friend, a loving friend and a friend who will give out the hand to help. Let us remember that Reuben was changed because he spoke to someone who he thought was just an ordinary plain shepherd, and yet he spoke to Christ.

To continue my story, Yes, It was true. I thought I was being very clever in bringing out the mastery of man, but I found that when the shepherd spoke to me I had such a wonderful feeling, a feeling that he was drawing me to him and, strangely enough, I was feeling afraid. It was the first time I had had the experience of being frightened.

I could not understand the change which came over me. It is true that I would have killed the rabbit. I have that rabbit with me now. Of course, the paw and his leg are alright now. There is nothing wrong with him. When I saw that rabbit so helpless, So much in pain, I felt that I could not kill it. I had killed many animals when I was young and was proud of it, but I realised that you can't be with God and be cruel to animals. Since I have been with Nicky, I have learnt a lot more. I have now gone with Nicky in a band to help many animals on your earth, but I do want to say to you, when you find little boys who are cruel, know that they just do not understand. Try to talk to them as the shepherd spoke to me because, although I have never since had that experience, I know I was talking to Christ and the Love of Jesus. I want to be able to do that again because I am not being opposite to Jesus. I am with Him. When you are with Him, you do not see Him, you only feel Him. It is only when you are opposite to Jesus that He might just transfigure somewhere. Now I am happy and the master of all situations by doing what He would have done.

EIGHTEEN

ROMANCE
A STORY OF TRUE SPIRITUAL LOVE

How often have we heard, that truth is stranger than fiction. This true and beautiful love story spread through two incarnations, cannot but inspire upliftment and comfort to those Souls who perhaps in their present consciousness of this life, feel a little neglected, not having found the fulfillment of a true love.

This modern fairytale story, is of a pretty young girl christened Catherine. Her parents were well placed in a material sense, and she spent a happy childhood, developing a great love of animals, especially horses. She was encouraged to be spiritually minded and to this day (although she is now a charming lady of almost 80 years young) has a very keen memory of the beautiful prayers her father used to say. In fact, she likes me to say special prayers for her now, as it reminds her so much of her father, whom she feels close to her at these times.

Whilst still young and engaged to be married, she accepted a position to work at a firm, and to her amazement found an instant deep attraction to the man who was her employer. Immediately he asked her to marry him, although he was many years her senior. She felt unable to accept him, because of her pervious standing engagement. He was tremendously kind to her, and they were linked in their daily work for seven years, when he became very sick and passed into the Spirit World. His name was Mark.

At one time, Catherine owned a riding school which brought her much joy, and her life was engrossed in the horses she loved so dearly. Her two special favourite horses were Monty and Shacks.

We came to know this charming lady about five years ago when she was brought by a friend, who had become attached to our Sanctuary, as a Spiritual Healer. Catherine was then in need of much help for a deep physical condition, and also in need of much mental upliftment. She

responded very well to the Spiritual healing and Spiritual teachings of truth which she received at "The White Chapel."
All her life she has kept Mark in her thoughts. He has always been very close to her spiritually and she has often sensed his presence. During some of the healings, Mark would try to take control so that he could speak to her, and although this was not permitted, I was able to relay intuitively direct messages from him to his love. This was a great joy to her. He has been waiting patiently thoughout her lifetime, for her to join him in Spirit, when her time comes to be called home. I had to speak strongly to them both at one time, because the tie was so strong between them that she was willing herself to leave the material life, before her time, so deteriorating physically. This is against God s' laws. One must wait for the appointed time to return to the eternal home of spiritual perfection.
One day, our Medium was assisting with the healing of Catherine, and had a beautiful vision, which was brought for her. It was of a huge white mansion, with four beautiful white pillars in front, a huge verandah and a large flight of white steps leading up to the mansion. Spacious, beautifully kept lawns in front, across which Catherine and Mark were walking, hand in hand, towards the house, followed by a big white dog. Away to the right of the house was a paddock filled with horses of every description, including the two which had been the special favourites of Catherine; Monty and Shacks.
This is the mansion which Mark has built for them in Spirit. It was also his home in a previous life, in which their two Souls were also brought together for a brief time. In this past life too, they had been deeply in love, but she was very young and her parents moved away from the district, taking her with them. They never met again in that life and he never married.
When Catherine had her 79th birthday, a special party was arranged for her by the friend who first brought her to the Sanctuary. Our Medium was present, and we all went into the Sanctuary in this friend s home, that Catherine might receive a special Blessing.
It was indeed a special Blessing and such a great joy for her. Her beloved Mark controlled the Medium and spoke to Catherine. Such a tender and touching reunion; it was difficult for all not to feel emotional.
He said, "I am happy to be able to penetrate this Medium so I may convey the wonder and beautiful pleasure of being Spirit. I want to know

if you are aware of whom I am?"
Norah and Catherine both said: "You are Mark."
(Mark then indicated that Catherine should put her hands in his, and make the contact).
"Yes, I am Mark. and you will always be 'My Bonnie Lass'. I think you are still beautiful, and have never left you throughout the years. I await the day when we will be united and you know I shall be there when that time arrives. You will be jubilant to find you know many that are here very well. We will go and travel many lands and through many vibrations. We shall again live in a beautiful mansion and have what was denied to us. We shall gather together in a union of power and love. I bless you until you yourself shall see me. I loved getting your thoughts directed to me. Let this be a beginning of a different world and a different life. Remember I wait patiently, as we cannot alter the time or the plan. Just know I shall never pass your door without taking a peep at you. Bless you, my darling, and know you shall always be as beautful as ever to me. Be at peace and be strong and know the tlme will soon come.
I wish to bless the lady of this Sanctuary. I have had a little difficulty in coming through today, but have managed it. May I wish you great success in your achievement. To Norah, I send my deepest love, which goes out to her Sanctuary. I have now accomplished what I desired since I passed into Spirit. We wait patitently for the day."

Norah asked: "May we come to the Wedding?"

Mark replied: "You know you are all invited. Then to my darling Bonnie Lass - remember I shall not leave you and shall be with you always."

Catherine then thanked Mark for coming and for the wonderful surprise. Since this meeeting Catherine has repeatedly said that it was the happiest birthday she has ever known.
We have been informed by the Medium's control, whom we call Padre (who has his own Chapel in Spirit) that when Catherine returns into Spirit, and after she has had a short rest, she and Mark will be linked together as one for all time, in a beautiful Spiritual Wedding. This has always been the desire within the Soul of each one. It could not be so in their material lives, but what a glorious ending. Not a fairy story, but an eternal perfect love together.

NINETEEN

MIND POWER

It has been seen how the power of the mind can influence life, when you return to your real home in Spirit.
Jesus said "The greatest power in heaven and earth, is the power of thought." Knowing that as we think so we are, our lives here on earth are similarly controlled.
We are Spirit in a material body now, and our minds are part of God's mind. God is Spirit, the Universal Mind is God. Therefore, we have this great power, we cannot escape from; even the air which we breathe is God Mind, Spiritual Vibration. How do we use this wonderful creative power?
Knowing we always have freedom of choice. Learn to expect that which you desire. Build in good faith, be it for good or negative, it must take form, it must take life. Know that which you create must come to pass, from the smallest to the biggest. Truth knows only that which is perfect. Thought is active, alive.
Close the door on yesterday, it is finished, and cannot be recalled today. There is only the present and the future. The life span is extremely short, in comparison with Spirit, which is eternal. adjust the mind in the positive direction of Divine Spirit; the power to lovingly create and build your life on a solid foundation. Clear the mind of confusion and obstacles, they can lead you nowhere.

TWENTY

THINK AND SPEAK IN POSITIVE PERFECTION

A mind that is confused is blind, blind to all light and enlightenment. The enlightenment which leads and keeps you on the right path, where nothing can hold you back. Take the Father God as your partner, with such assurance, you cannot go astray. Building your life on your own foundation of negativeness, you will always fall, it has no power, except to destroy.

In creating a positive image of all you desire, you will find that beautiful peace that passeth all understanding.

TWENTY ONE

PRAYER

Oh Great White Spirit, Loving Father, Our All. Our Loving Father who created all the universe and all therein in beauty and perfection, designed to live, and there to thrive in a vibration of love and peace.
We, thy children, continue to stray, even though we can see your ever constant presence and unfailing promises in your perfect laws of life, which never change or tire.
Let us sing a song of praise from within the heart unto Him who has created us, in His Image.
Each morning as the golden glow of the sun lightens up the Eastern sky, bringing warmth; may we be lifted up by the thrill of life, which quickens every tree, plant and blade of grass. All creatures of the earth awakening with joyous voices to welcome the symbol of divine energy of light, life and love.
So we give forth a prayer of thanks to Him who created all the wonders of the universe, giving His life to all, through all forms -to express His love divine. May we realise the oneness of our being with great and small linked by the unity of love. That Peace Divine may penetrate the heart, a peace we may send forth into the heart and mind of every child to radiate to all creation.
As the Christ love wells up within the heart and embracing all life, that all may share the ectasy, aware of the vibration of the indwelling spirit, in deep humility to claim "Oh Father, I am at one with every atom in the universe."
May our Father's great power of life, love and peace fill our hearts and minds now and for all eternity.
Thank you Father.
AMEN

TWENTY TWO

A MESSAGE FROM JESUS

My beloved children of this Earth, come unto me. I will protect you and I will guide you for I love you. I see not the temptations that are placed before you, I see only you. The Spirit, the Perfection, the Divine Love, the complete freedom. I guide you into the realms of safety. I guide you my children into the harbour where you will find peace.
The peace that I bring to you so freely, so filled with love. Come unto me that I may help you find the inner peace which is the Spirit. The Life, the Light and the Way. To each one, it matters not what colour, creed or religion, each one is a Temple in which I dwell. I beseech you my Beloved children, seek and find and to come unto me. Blessed are you who shall find me, Blessed are you who will surely know the Divine Light. May the Light of Purification ever be your guide through your imaginary darkness upon your Earth.
For as ye seek the light you will find the upliftment of Divine Spirit.